Teatime Tillie

Tate Publishing & Enterprises

Carla Rae Johnson

Published by Tate Publishing & Enterprises, LLC
127 E. Trade Center Terrace | Mustang, Oklahoma 73064 USA
1.888.361.9473 | www.tatepublishing.com

Tate Publishing is committed to excellence in the publishing industry. The company reflects the philosophy established by the founders, based on Psalm 68:11,
"The Lord gave the word and great was the company of those who published it."

Book design copyright © 2010 by Tate Publishing, LLC. All rights reserved.
Cover and Interior design by Michael Lee
Illustration by Kurt Jones

Published in the United States of America

ISBN: 978-1-61663-122-2
1. Juvenile Fiction: Animals: Mice
2. Juvenile Fiction: Cooking & Food
10.04.16

To my favorite teatime chums—
Amy, Andrew, Annie, Christian, and Abigail

There was a young mouse who loved to take tea.

She primped and she prepped and she giggled with glee.

Tillie was her name, and she had friends that she loved.
She was ever so gentle, as sweet as a dove.
"Teatime is an event that makes me feel blessed,
a time to refresh and a time to de-stress!"

As she went about her preparations
with tenderness and care,
Tillie remembered each friend
with a soft, little prayer.

"Bless Alice and Nettie, Stacy and Rosie.
Let my house be warm and comfy and cozy."

Tillie baked and dusted, sorted and mopped.
She did it for love and not to show off.
"The best part of teatime is sipping the tea
and enjoying my friends with kind hospitality."

Teatime arrived, and Tillie was ready.
She greeted her friends Stacy, Rosie, Alice, and Nettie.
"Sit down to my table. I hope it brings joy.
Share a cuppa sweet friendship without being coy."

The wee friends snickered, and chattered,
and felt very chummy,
as each munched on sweet morsels
and patted her tummy.

"The sun has stopped shining. I fear it will rain.
I must rescue my laundry and protect it from stain."
So off Alice scuttled, warm words of thanks on her lips.
That left just four at the table to take the last sips.

Then, just as Miss Tillie stood to pour more tea,
Nettie sweetly excused herself, and then there were three.
The three small companions snuggled in for a chat,
when Stacy remembered she'd lost her best hat.

"I must return to my home to look and to search.
I wish to wear my lovely hat next Sunday to church."
So with a wave, and a wink, and a fond "adieu,"
little Stacy tottered off, and then there were two.

Two is a nice number to settle in for the day,
but soon quiet Rosie was anxious to be on her way.
"My grandma is sick. I'll take her a sweet bun."
Rosie waved good-bye and then there was one.

The day was a busy one, but Tillie was content.
She'd been blessed by her friends and
knew what love meant.

To be alone in her snug, little house just couldn't be.
Because she'd invited her very best friend
for the last cup of tea!

A friend loves at all times
Proverbs 17:17a

e|LIVE

listen|imagine|view|experience

AUDIO BOOK DOWNLOAD INCLUDED WITH THIS BOOK!

In your hands you hold a complete digital entertainment package. Besides purchasing the paper version of this book, this book includes a free download of the audio version of this book. Simply use the code listed below when visiting our website. Once downloaded to your computer, you can listen to the book through your computer's speakers, burn it to an audio CD or save the file to your portable music device (such as Apple's popular iPod) and listen on the go!

How to get your free audio book digital download:

1. Visit www.tatepublishing.com and click on the e|LIVE logo on the home page.
2. Enter the following coupon code:
   70b7-7abb-62b5-74a4-d916-696a-ce5a-19fb

3. Download the audio book from your e|LIVE digital locker and begin enjoying your new digital entertainment package today!